Apple Juice Tea

by Martha Weston

CLARION BOOKS / *New York*

Clarion Books
a Houghton Mifflin Company imprint
215 Park Avenue South, New York, NY 10003
Text and illustrations copyright © 1994 by Martha Weston

The illustrations for this book were executed in pen and ink and watercolor
on Windsor & Newton hot press watercolor paper
The text is set in 14/17 pt. Garamond Book

For information about permission to reproduce selections from this book,
write to Permissions, Houghton Mifflin Company,
215 Park Avenue South, New York, NY 10003.

Printed in the U.S.A.

Library of Congress Cataloging-in-Publication Data

Weston, Martha.
    Apple juice tea / by Martha Weston.
        p.   cm.
    Summary: When Gran comes to visit, Polly wishes she would go home,
until one night when Gran babysits.
    ISBN 0-395-65480-7
    [1. Grandmothers—Fiction.]   I. Title.
    PZ7.W52645Ap   1994
    [E]—dc20   93-17437
                                                                         CIP
                                                                         AC

BVG   10 9 8 7 6 5 4 3 2 1

For Dory and her Gran,
the original tea party pair

Polly has a mama, a daddy, and a gran. Polly's gran lives far away. Now she is coming to visit.

"You were a tiny baby the last time you saw Gran," says Mama. "Do you remember her?"

Polly sees Gran's picture in the hall every day. She thinks she remembers Gran a little bit.

Gran comes on a big plane. Mama says it's Gran, and Daddy says it's Gran, but her face doesn't look like her picture in the hall. "I have a hug for you, Polly," says Gran. But Polly doesn't know Gran, and she doesn't want Gran to hug her.

At home, Polly wants to be with Mama, but Mama is always talking to Gran.

At the zoo, Gran says, "Will you show me the gorillas, Polly?"
"I always see gorillas with Daddy," says Polly.

At the park, Gran says, "Want a push on the swing, Polly?"
"Mama always pushes me on the swing," says Polly.

At bedtime, Daddy says, "Let Gran read you *The Three Bears,* Polly."

"No!" says Polly. "I don't want a story."

She wishes it could just be Polly and Mama and Daddy and that's all.

But the next morning when Polly gets up, Gran is still there.

Gran has made buttery, warm biscuits. Polly is eating one when Mama says, "Polly, Daddy and I are going out tonight, and Gran is going to baby-sit you."

"But Ellie is my baby-sitter," says Polly. "I want Ellie to come."

"Ellie is busy and Gran wants to help. I'm sure you'll have a good time," says Mama.

"We could have a tea party tonight, Polly," says Gran.

"No we couldn't," says Polly.

"Why not?" asks Mama.

"Pretty Doll and Mr. Bun always spill their tea," says Polly.

"How about if you and I have apple juice tea and Mr. Bun and Pretty Doll have macaroni tea?" asks Gran.

"Maybe," says Polly.

After supper it's time to hug Mama and Daddy goodbye. Polly holds on tight. Then she runs to her room and shuts the door. She doesn't want Gran to help her put on her pajamas.

After a while, Gran peeks in. "I don't want a tea party," says Polly.

"Okay," says Gran. "What *do* you want to do, Polly?"

Polly looks out the window. It is starting to get dark. She hears crickets. "I want to take Pretty Doll and Mr. Bun for a walk," she says. She is sure Gran will say, "Not now, honey, it's bedtime."

But Gran says, "Okay."

"Really?" Polly can't believe it. "In my pajamas?"

"Sure," says Gran.

Polly gets her slippers and puts Mr. Bun and Pretty Doll in her old stroller. "I'm going to the corner. I'll be back soon," she tells Gran.

Polly starts walking down the sidewalk. Soon she comes to the bump in the cement where she tripped once and skinned her knee. She wants to show this to Gran. Polly calls to Gran, "You come too, okay?"

Gran joins her. Polly shows Gran the sidewalk bump. She shows her the blackberry bushes and the neighbors' cat.

It is a warm night. They walk up to the corner and back down, talking the whole time.

Back on her doorstep, Polly has an idea. "Wait!" she tells Gran. "I will go in first. Then you knock. You are my visitor."

Polly goes inside and shuts the door. Soon there is a knock.

"Who is it?" calls Polly.

"It's Gran. I've come to visit you," Gran calls back.

Polly opens the door. "Okay, come in! Would you like some tea?"

Gran has a big smile. "Oh, yes I would, thank you," she says.

They go into the kitchen. Polly gets a big tray and Gran puts apple juice, cups, and saucers on it. Polly pours dry macaroni into little cups for Mr. Bun and Pretty Doll.

Gran starts to put the tray on the big table.

"Yoo-hoo, Gran!" says Polly. "I'm down here! Let's have tea in my table house."

So Gran and Polly have an apple juice tea party under the big table. Polly decides she likes the way Gran holds her cup and saucer. She tries to hold hers the same way.

It is past Polly's bedtime when she crawls under the covers and listens to Gran read *The Three Little Pigs*. Gran has a funny, squeaky pig voice and a deep, growly wolf voice. Then Gran sings a lullaby that Polly has never heard before. It is a long one, a little sweet and a little sad. While Gran is singing, Polly falls asleep.

24

The next morning, Gran is still there. Polly and Gran go to the store together to buy more apple juice.

That afternoon they have a tea party on the back steps . . .

and the day after that, a tea party in Polly's room.

Then the day comes when Gran has to go home. Polly, Mama, and Daddy take her to the airport.

"I have a hug for you," says Polly.

Now Polly misses Gran. She gets her crayons and draws a picture of Polly, Gran, Pretty Doll, and Mr. Bun having an apple juice tea party.

She mails it to Gran.

One day, an envelope comes for Polly. It's from Gran. Inside is a picture of Gran. In the picture she is holding a teacup and smiling.

Polly takes the new picture to the hall. She holds it up next to the old one. "Now I remember Gran," Polly tells Mama. "*This* is Gran. My tea party Gran."